Dear Parent:
Your child's love of reading starts here!

Every child learns to read in a different way and at his or her own speed. Some go back and forth between reading levels and read favorite books again and again. Others read through each level in order. You can help your young reader improve and become more confident by encouraging his or her own interests and abilities. From books your child reads with you to the first books he or she reads alone, there are I Can Read Books for every stage of reading:

SHARED READING
Basic language, word repetition, and whimsical illustrations, ideal for sharing with your emergent reader

BEGINNING READING
Short sentences, familiar words, and simple concepts for children eager to read on their own

READING WITH HELP
Engaging stories, longer sentences, and language play for developing readers

READING ALONE
Complex plots, challenging vocabulary, and high-interest topics for the independent reader

ADVANCED READING
Short paragraphs, chapters, and exciting themes for the perfect bridge to chapter books

I Can Read Books have introduced children to the joy of reading since 1957. Featuring award-winning authors and illustrators and a fabulous cast of beloved characters, I Can Read Books set the standard for beginning readers.

A lifetime of discovery begins with the magical words "I Can Read!"

Visit www.icanread.com for information
on enriching your child's reading experience.

I Can Read Book® is a trademark of HarperCollins Publishers.

Flat Stanley and the Lost Treasure
Text copyright © 2016 by the Trust u/w/o Richard C. Brown a/k/a Jeff Brown f/b/o Duncan Brown.
Illustrations by Macky Pamintuan, copyright © 2016 by HarperCollins Publishers.
All rights reserved. Manufactured in the U.S.A. No part of this book may be used or reproduced in any manner whatsoever without
written permission except in the case of brief quotations embodied in critical articles and reviews. For information address
HarperCollins Children's Books, a division of HarperCollins Publishers, 195 Broadway, New York, NY 10007.
www.icanread.com
Library of Congress Control Number: 2015950814
ISBN 978-0-06-236596-5 (trade bdg.)—ISBN 978-0-06-236595-8 (pbk.)
Typography by Jeff Shake

16 17 18 19 20 LSCC 10 9 8 7 6 5 4 3 2   ❖   First Edition

FLAT STANLEY
and the Lost Treasure

created by Jeff Brown
by Lori Haskins Houran
pictures by Macky Pamintuan

HARPER

An Imprint of HarperCollinsPublishers

Stanley Lambchop lived
with his mother,
his father,
and his little brother, Arthur.

Stanley was four feet tall,

about a foot wide,

and half an inch thick.

He had been flat ever since

a bulletin board fell on him.

Sometimes being flat was great.

Especially on trips.

Stanley could fold himself up

and get comfy anywhere.

Stanley could roll himself up
and catch a ride, too.
"I wouldn't mind a ride,"
grumbled Arthur.

But being flat on the beach

was a pain in the neck.

And the leg, and the arm . . .

"Ouch!" cried Stanley.

"That's the third time

I've been stepped on today!"

Stanley brushed off the sand.

"Let's do something else,"

he said to Arthur.

"Want to go snorkeling?"

"Sure!" said Arthur.

"Stay in the cove,"
Mrs. Lambchop called.
"Okay," the boys agreed,
pulling on their masks.

Stanley splashed into the sea.

"Last one in is a rotten egg!"

"No fair!" said Arthur.

"You don't have to put on fins!"

Stanley grinned.

"It's not my fault

I have them built in!"

Stanley's flat feet helped him swim
faster than Arthur.

But he didn't mind slowing down.

There was so much to see!

Stanley spotted a school

of bright blue fish.

Arthur pointed out a stingray.

"Hey! It's flat like you!"

he tried to say.

But it sounded like,

"Glub! Gla glub glub glub!"

A small silver dolphin

zipped past Stanley.

It whirled around and swam back,

so close he could almost touch it.

Swish!

The dolphin raced ahead again.

It looked back at the boys

as if it wanted them to come along!

Stanley looked at Arthur.

Arthur nodded eagerly.

The boys kicked hard and followed

the dolphin to the end of the cove.

Below them, the ocean floor dipped.
There, nestled on the bottom,
lay an old ship!

The dolphin dived down.

The boys took deep breaths

and dived, too.

They couldn't believe what they saw.

The ship's sails were torn.

Its nets were tangled.

But in the middle of the wreck

sat a chest of gleaming gold!

Stanley kicked back to the surface.

Arthur's head popped up next to him.

"Did you see that?" Arthur cried.

"Let's grab a bunch of gold.

We'll be rich!"

"Hold on," said Stanley.

"That treasure must belong

to somebody.

Let's take one piece

to show everyone.

Then we'll figure out what to do."

"Aw, okay," said Arthur.

Just then, a wave slapped Stanley.

Then another.

"It's getting choppy," he said.

"I think it's going to storm.

Wait here, Arthur.

I'll hurry and get the gold!"

Stanley dived to the ship again.

He picked up a gold bar.

It was the size of a candy bar,

but much heavier!

He slid it into the pocket

of his trunks.

Stanley was about to head back up

when he saw the dolphin.

Its tail was caught

in an old fishing net on the ship!

"I've got to help," thought Stanley,

"before we both run out of breath!"

Quickly Stanley rolled himself up.

He tried to slide through a hole

in the net.

But something got stuck.

The gold bar!

Stanley yanked it out of his pocket

and tossed it away.

Now Stanley fit easily into the net.

He used his flat fingers to pry

the rope off the dolphin's tail.

The little dolphin was free!

Seconds later, Stanley burst

out of the water.

He took a big gulp of fresh air.

Beside him, the dolphin

whistled softly.

"You're welcome," said Stanley.

"Stanley!" yelled Arthur. "Help!"
The water wasn't just choppy now.
The wind was whipping it
into wild waves!

"Jump on, Arthur!" Stanley called.

He threw himself on a wave

like a surfboard!

"Woo-hoo!" cried Arthur.

The boys rode the waves

all the way to shore.

By morning, the storm had passed.

Stanley and Arthur took

their parents to see the shipwreck.

"It was here. Really!" said Stanley.

Mr. and Mrs. Lambchop peered

into the water.